# WHAT'S HAPPENED
# TO HARRY?

The Beast in the Bed
The Good-Guy Cake
Who Needs a Bear?

Barbara Dillon

# WHAT'S HAPPENED TO HARRY?

ILLUSTRATED BY
CHRIS CONOVER
William Morrow and Company
New York   1982

Printed in the United States of America.
1  2  3  4  5  6  7  8  9  10

Library of Congress Cataloging in Publication Data

Dillon, Barbara.
    What's happened to Harry?
    Summary: Harry becomes entangled with a witch on Halloween night and is transformed into a poodle.
    [1. Witches—Fiction. 2. Halloween—Fiction] I. Conover, Chris, ill.  II. Title.
PZ7.D57916Wh  [Fic]  81-11153
ISBN 0-688-00763-5      AACR2

To Harry, of course.

# CONTENTS

# CHAPTER ONE

# HALLOWEEN NIGHT

n Halloween afternoon, Harry Clooney ran all the way home from school. He could hardly wait to see the costume that his mother had promised to pick up for him that morning.

"I'm going to be either Red Raider or Black Bandit," he had told his friends, "whichever one Stoler's can order for me in my size."

Either costume would be great, Harry thought, as he ran up the driveway. Excitedly he imagined himself in the long scarlet cape of Red Raider or the tight-fitting ebony mask and shiny plastic boots of Black Bandit.

"Which one did you get?" he asked his mother breathlessly, as he pushed open the kitchen door.

Mrs. Clooney, who was chopping onion at the sink, wiped her hands silently on her apron before she turned to look at her son. "Harry, sit down and have a Twinkie," she advised, handing him one from a box on top of the refrigerator.

"Where's my costume?" Harry asked again, plunking himself down at the kitchen table.

"Well, there was a kind of a mix-up at Stoler's," said his mother, looking nervous.

"What kind of a mix-up?" Harry demanded, laying the unwrapped Twinkie on the table.

"The only costume they received today in

your size was a—a French poodle," his mother told him. The expression on her face was like that of someone trying to cross a stream on small, slippery stones without falling in.

"A poodle!" Harry exploded. "That's a costume for babies! I'm not gonna wear it!" But he knew even as he protested that it was much too late to come up with anything else. He would be a poodle or nothing.

He certainly didn't feel any better, either, when several hours later, his sister, Lolly, getting her first look at him in his one-piece dog suit with a fluffy poodle tail stitched onto the seat, burst out laughing.

"Maybe you should carry your trick-or-treat bag in your mouth," she said with a giggle, smug in her Bo Peep costume. "Maybe someone will offer you Dog Yummies."

"Shut up, you," said Harry bitterly, making a pass at her frilly blue bonnet.

"Children, children," said Mr. Clooney, stepping in between them, "let's not start Halloween night with a fight. I want you both to have a good time and to bring home lots of loot. Remember, chocolate-covered

marshmallows are your father's favorite."
He paused for a moment, looking from one
to the other. "Home by eight thirty," he reminded them, "and stay away from the
Blackburn place."

"Don't worry, Dad," said Lolly, picking
up her trick-or-treat bag from the hall table.
"Anybody'd have to be crazy to go to a
haunted house, especially on Halloween."

Harry looked pityingly at his sister
through his poodle mask.

"You really believe that place is haunted,
don't you?" he asked. "Just because dopey
Beezy Brinkerhoff imagined she saw a
face looking out of a window one day."

"She did see a face," Lolly insisted. "It
was lopsided and was mushroom-colored,
and the nose was pressed all flat against the
windowpane."

"Boy, what an imagination!" scoffed
Harry.

"And besides," said Lolly, "other people have seen strange things too, and you know it."

Harry had, in fact, like everyone else in town, heard some intriguing reports about the Blackburn place. Lou Gade, the mailman, reported having seen a face too, but this time it was a man's with a bushy black beard. And old Mr. Simmons, who lived two doors away from the Blackburn place, insisted that one night he had seen a wavering light inside the empty house, a light that looked like a candle being carried from room to room.

"The place is empty. No one's lived there for years," Harry insisted. But he couldn't help asking, "Dad, there's no such thing as a haunted house, is there?"

"Of course not," his father assured him. "But I still want you both to steer clear of the Blackburn place all the same."

He and Mrs. Clooney stood at the front door with their children. "It's the strangest darn weather," commented Mr. Clooney, staring up at the sky. "There hasn't been a breath of air stirring for weeks. I've never seen anything like it."

"Our weathervane's been pointing north since the middle of September!" said Mrs. Clooney, standing at his side. "And the old windmill at the end of the Grissolm property hasn't turned an inch in at least that long."

"Makes me uneasy," said Mr. Clooney. "It just isn't natural for the wind to disappear so completely and for so long. There's something very spooky about it."

The children ran eagerly down the front walk. Lolly turned right to meet her best friend, Beezy Brinkerhoff, and Harry veered left at a fast clip so as to get a head start on all his friends.

Out on Ring's End Road, Harry, quite for-getting about his disappointment with the poodle costume, was hurrying happily from house to house, stuffing his trick-or-treat bag with every goody that he was offered. When he received little boxes of raisins and small, tart apples, he muttered, "Yuck," under his mask but thanked the people politely anyway. At one house where chocolate-covered marshmallow bars were being handed out, he said, "Neato! Can I have an extra for my dad?"

From time to time he met friends dressed as ghosts and tramps and TV sets.

"I'm getting some really good stuff, you guys," he boasted. And then, lying a little in order to ward off any smart-aleck remarks about his costume, he added, "And I can stay out till midnight if I want."

"Guess what we saw," said the Goodhue twins, who were dressed as Tweedledum and Tweedledee. "A jack-o'-lantern in the window of the Blackburn place."

"You're kidding!" said Harry, his eyes widening in surprise. "Who do you suppose put it there?" And then he had a sudden bright idea. "Let's go and peek in, okay?"

The twins hesitated for a moment.

" 'Member Mr. Gade saw a man's face looking out of one of the windows last summer," Peter Goodhue reminded Harry nervously.

"It had a big, black beard," recalled his brother Eric.

"So what?" scoffed Harry. "What harm can there be just looking in a window?"

"None, I guess," agreed Peter uncertainly. And he and his brother, their padded stomachs bouncing up and down, scampered off after Harry, who was already running toward Swift's Lane.

When the three boys came in sight of the

Blackburn place, they all slowed down together, looking in awe at the house in front of them. Rising massively out of the velvety sky, it looked like a big storm cloud waiting to engulf anyone who came too close. The only glint of light was from the face of the fat, gap-toothed pumpkin grinning out at them from a downstairs window. Silently the boys crept up the front walk. By standing on tiptoe, they could just see over the windowsill into the room beyond.

"It's completely empty," announced Eric, stepping back from the window with relief. "Let's get out of here."

"Yikes!" cried Peter in sudden alarm. "That pumpkin just winked at me!" And he and his brother turned and tore down the front walk in a panic. Harry ran too, but not quite as fast; his curiosity about the Blackburn place and who had put the jack-o'-lantern in the window was now greater than ever.

"I think I'll just go back and ring the bell one time," he told the twins.

"You better not," warned Peter, glancing fearfully over his shoulder at the house. "There's something really bad about that place."

"Anyway, no one who goes out in a baby costume is about to go up and ring the bell of a haunted house," jeered Eric, feeling a little braver now that he was safely out on the street.

The remark about his costume really got to Harry. "Oh yeah? Well, watch this," he said, sounding very cool. He hoisted his trick-or-treat bag over his shoulder and swaggered back up the walk. Carefully he climbed the rickety steps to the front porch and lifted the handle of the big door knocker cast in the shape of a cat's head. With the first rap, the cat let out a loud, plaintive yowl. Harry withdrew his hand in alarm and turned to flee after the twins, whose footsteps he could hear slapping down the pavement of Swift's Lane. But at that moment the front door creaked open, and there on the threshold stood a little old lady dressed all in black except for a frilly white apron. She had curly white hair and twinkly spectacles perched on the end of her nose. When she saw Harry on the doorstep, she clapped her hands and laughed in delight.

"Well, if that isn't the cutest costume," she said, chuckling. "I think it deserves a very special treat. Come in, dear, come in." She reached out and with a surprisingly strong grip for anyone so tiny and so old drew him into the house.

Clutching his bag in both hands, Harry looked uneasily about him. He was standing in a dim, narrow hallway lit only by two sputtering black candles on a table to the right of the door. On top of the table rested a small glass globe—the kind that, when you shake it, produces a miniature snowstorm. But the extraordinary thing about this one was that the snow inside it was racing wildly around the tiny pine tree in the center of the globe, as if some invisible hand had just given it a vigorous shake. Seeing Harry's eyes fixed on the globe, the old lady reached out and snatched it quickly from the table.

"This globe is my most treasured possession," she told him, clutching it tightly in both hands. "When I'm at home, I always keep it out for show."

"How come the snow inside swirls around all by itself?" Harry asked.

"Ah, that *is* a puzzle, isn't it?" the old lady said with a mysterious smile. "A real conundrum. But let's not worry our heads about it just now." Placing the globe back on the table with exaggerated care, she took Harry by the arm and propelled him rapidly down the dark hallway.

Harry, stumbling along, gave a long shiver. It sure is cold in here, he thought, cold and clammy like the inside of a cave.

At that moment, he wished mightily that he had listened to his father and not come anywhere near the Blackburn place.

Uneasily he glanced into the two big rooms on either side of the hall. Although they both appeared to be empty, the archways leading into them were festooned with webs. In one sat a fat black spider, who waggled a leg at him as he passed. Harry stared back in amazement. Could it possibly be a pet spider? he wondered. But the old lady was pushing him impatiently ahead of her.

"Here we are," she announced, pausing at the entrance to a big, old-fashioned kitchen. Harry peered in cautiously. At one end of the room was a stone fireplace in which a cheerful fire crackled; at the other end stood a massive cupboard with double doors. Harry glanced quickly at both. But what caught his attention and held it was a long, wooden table in the center of the room. Spread out on top of the table was the most sumptuous display of sweets Harry had ever seen in his life. There was a shiny glass bowl filled with caramels and next to it a plate of fudge squares and maple sugar nuggets and his father's favorite chocolate-covered marshmallows. There was a tray piled high with shiny, red candy apples, and beside it stood a tall pyramid of crunchy popcorn balls. There were baskets filled with peppermints and stacks of all-day suckers in every flavor. There were yards and yards of red and black licorice whips. There were slabs of white chocolate and dark chocolate and platters of sparkling gumdrops and pink candy hearts and nougats and nuts and butterscotch balls. And

in the center of the table was a large basket woven of shimmering strands of spun sugar that was filled with candies shaped and colored like flowers and fruits.

"Oh, wow!" was all Harry could say, as he gazed in rapture at the wondrous display before him. But as he stepped eagerly across

the threshold of the room, a green parrot with a dagger-sharp beak suddenly swooped toward him from atop the big cupboard.

"Dumbbell, dumbbell," the bird gabbled, looking at Harry with bright, inquisitive eyes.

"Don't mind Black Bart," the old lady chortled. "He's completely daft and rude as they come." And she flapped her apron irritably at the bird, driving him back to his cupboard perch where he paced from side to side, murmuring and clucking to himself and never taking his eyes off Harry.

The old lady, smiling and nodding, led Harry gently to the kitchen table.

"Don't be shy, help yourself. Take as much as you can carry," she urged him. She rubbed her hands together and said "Attaboy" as she watched Harry greedily cram his bag with fistfuls of delectable treats.

When at last his sack was filled to overflowing, she stepped swiftly in front of him.

"Why don't you have one for the road?" she suggested. "Here, try one of these sugar babies. They're my favorite." She picked up a candy and held it out to Harry. Harry pushed back his mask with one hand and popped the candy into his mouth with the other.

"Aha," exclaimed the old lady, peering admiringly into his face. "Curly hair, brown eyes and freckles—my favorite combination." She smiled and gave him a big wink.

"Now I bet you didn't know that I'm wearing a mask too," she said.

Harry looked at her, puzzled. "I don't see any mask," he said, munching on his sugar baby.

With that, the old lady reached out and grasped his arm. "Let me show you something wonderful," she said, dragging him over to the big cupboard. With her free hand she dug into the pocket of her apron and drew out a small, gold key, which she inserted into the lock.

"Dumbbell, dumbbell," croaked the parrot, swooping to the windowsill, where he paced agitatedly back and forth on his matchstick legs and continued to cluck at Harry.

The old lady pulled open the cupboard door and took a step backward. "Behold," she said in a commanding voice.

Nervously Harry peeked into the shadowy interior. There, dangling limply from pegs nailed in the walls, he saw what looked like a lot of big puppets. There was a witch with an ancient, shriveled face and a trailing black cape sewn with big pockets, from one of which hopped a bumpy-skinned horned toad. There was a pirate with a cutlass clamped in his teeth and a curly black beard; there was a pretty cheerleader with long, blond hair and a nurse and a clown and a tramp. There was even a pink, rubbery-looking baby in a flannel nightgown.

"What are they?" Harry asked, staring open-mouthed.

"What were they, you mean," said the old lady with a laugh. "They were mortals once, just like you—except, of course, for this beauty." She reached into the cupboard and lovingly drew forth the witch form.

"This is the *real* me!" she cried, flourishing the form in front of Harry. "The fantastic, flamboyant, fabulous me." And the little old lady rapidly swirled the witch's cape about her skinny shoulders so that for a second it looked as if she had been swallowed up by an enormous black crow. Harry blinked in astonishment as a second later, a clawlike hand lifted the edge of the cape, disclosing the hideous, grinning face of the witch.

"Hepzibah the Hateful, at your service,"
she chortled, tilting the brim of her witch's
hat jauntily over one eyebrow. Then she
bent down and gathered up the old lady
form that lay at her feet like a crumpled

paper doll and hung it neatly in the cupboard next to the pirate.

Harry didn't need to see any more to convince him that he was in deep trouble. "I want to go home!" he wailed, struggling to free himself from the witch's iron grip. "I want to go home right now!"

"All in good time," cackled Hepzibah, "all in good time. But we have some business to take care of first. Can you guess what it is?"

Harry thrust his trick-or-treat bag toward her hopefully. But he knew she wanted more from him than Halloween loot.

"I don't want your candy, you ninny," snarled the witch. "It's your face I want for my costume collection. Your face and your nice, sturdy boy's body."

"You're kidding!" croaked Harry.

"I'm deadly serious," Hepzibah assured him.

"But why?" whimpered Harry. "Why?"

"Why?" said Hepzibah. "Why not? I like costumes. I like disguises. Variety is the spice of life, you know. Even a witch can get bored with being the same old spook. Besides, it is my sacred mission to bug mortals. It is my life's work to give them a tough time. And what better way than to get inside their skins?" With a gleeful laugh, she lifted the cheerleader form from the cupboard. Demurely she held it up in front of her so Harry could get the effect.

"Rickety rack! Rickety rack! Come on team, and push 'em back," she yelled. Giggling, she draped the form over the back of a kitchen chair.

"One whole fall I was head cheerleader at Henry Livingston High," she told Harry. "I really had a ball. At the big game against Prudden Prep, I managed, with a quickie spell, to tie the other girls' shoelaces together, so when they jumped up to give a cheer, they all fell flat on their faces. The crowd loved it! So did I. And then"—Hepzibah began cackling uncontrollably—"before the state championship, I rubbed the football with a little oil of newt. Nobody could hold on to it. That ball was squirting out of players' hands like toothpaste out of a tube. The teams were cursing, the coaches were going nuts, it was beautiful." Wiping the tears of merriment from her eyes, she reached out and took the nurse down from her peg in the cupboard.

"When I feel like wreaking havoc in a hospital, I wear this," Hepzibah explained. "Sometimes, on a slow night, I get suited up and appear for night duty. I smash thermometers, change stuff on patients' charts, do a few cute tricks in the medicine cabinets. Oh, the possibilities over there at Stokes Memorial are endless."

Harry looked around the kitchen in desperation. He had to find a way to escape while there was still time, he simply had to.

"Don't worry," Hepzibah was saying, "it's only your body I'm after. You get to keep your silly heart and your batty brains."

"But what's the good of a heart and a brain with no body to keep them in?" asked Harry in a trembling voice.

"Oh, you'll have a body all right," Hepzibah assured him. "Not quite what you're used to, of course, but nevertheless a body."

"I don't understand," said Harry weakly.

"Well," drawled Hepzibah, "let me see if I can explain." She reached in the cupboard and gave the pirate's limp arm a playful flick with her finger.

"One of my oldest victims," she said. "When I snitched his skin, I decided to stuff what was left in a bird body." She raised her eyes to the windowsill, where the parrot was hunched dejectedly. "Guess who?" she snickered.

"Dumbbell, dumbbell," said the bird, looking mournfully at Harry.

"The nurse I decided to stick in a spider suit," said Hepzibah. "You may have noticed her working on her web in the hallway. The baby, crazy, kindhearted crone that I am, I placed inside a kitten skin. It's so much easier for the mother to take care of than a drooling, yowling baby. As for the others"—Hepzibah shrugged and yawned as if the subject was beginning to bore her— "I turned them into bats or butterflies or whatever. The tramp, if I remember correctly, became a flea-bitten old hound dog, the clown, a performing seal." She suddenly frowned and gave Harry's arm a painful squeeze. "But enough of this chitter-chatter," she said briskly. "Let's get the show on the road." Then Hepzibah closed her eyes, and a dreamy look stole over her evil face. Weaving back and forth, jerking Harry to and fro with her, she began to chant:

"Pumpkin pits and witches' wits,
Masks and cats and big, black bats.
Halloween night to me brings joy,
But not to you, unlucky boy.
Your day has come, your day has gone,
'Tis just as if you'd ne'er been born.
A boy again you'll never be.
Your skin, your shape belong to me."

"No," cried Harry, beating at Hepzibah with his fist. "No, I won't let you!" But even as he spoke, there was a strange humming in his ears. The fire in the fireplace suddenly flared up, lighting the kitchen with an unholy red glow, and the witch seemed to be growing rapidly taller. Either that or he was getting shorter. "No!" he screamed again, pulling away from her with all his strength.

36

Suddenly Hepzibah let go of Harry's arm, sending him flipping backward, head over heels. He felt as though he had been knocked over by a big wave and couldn't tell where his head or feet were or in which direction he was facing. When he finally managed to scramble dizzily upright, he found, to his joy, that he was no longer in the witch's kitchen but outside on the front lawn.

"I've escaped," he cried. But horribly, unbelievably, what came out of his mouth were not words but woofs! A rush of terror swept over Harry. He looked fearfully down at his toes and discovered they had been replaced by silky, black paws. Beneath his chin was a furry dog chest. Lolling from his mouth was the tip of a long, pink tongue.

"Holy moly, she's done it to me!" Harry moaned. "She's turned me into a poodle!"

"Help, help!" he barked, as he fled in

panic down Swift's Lane. But of course there was no one—no one at all—who could come to his aid. Blindly he ran on, scarcely noticing where he was going, his mind in a turmoil as it leaped from one awful thought to another.

They won't recognize me at home, he grieved, and after a while they'll all think I'm dead, and Mom'll be so sad, and Lolly will get my new poster paints. And then something really terrible occurred to him as he rounded the corner. All his friends were going to grow up without him. They would become baseball players and pilots and space scientists while he remained forever a French poodle. And no more decent Christmas presents either, he realized with a pang. He'd be lucky this year even to get a rubber bone.

A sudden snapping of twigs in back of him made Harry jump. He glanced over his shoulder and imagined he saw a dark shape slip behind a tree. Nervously he again broke into a gallop. Enough bad things had happened to him for one night. He certainly didn't want to meet up with any more spooks —ever.

# CHAPTER TWO

# HARRY
# THE POODLE

ook at this beautiful dog, Dad!" Harry's sister cried when, a few moments later, Harry scratched at the Clooneys' front door.

"I am more interested in boys than dogs," said Mr. Clooney, as Lolly let Harry into the hall. "It's almost nine o'clock and still no sign of your brother."

Harry discovered his mother sitting by the fireplace with her mending. He bounced across the room to her side and put his front paws in her lap.

"I'm Harry. I'm your son," he told her imploringly. But of course only whines and woofs came out.

Mrs. Clooney dropped her mending to pat the strange dog. She looked into his sweet brown eyes, and her face became thoughtful. "It's weird," she said, "but something about him reminds me of Harry."

"I am Harry, I am!" Harry whimpered, licking his mother's cheek with his new long tongue.

"Oh, Mom, he's so cute, can we keep him?" begged Lolly. "He won't be any trouble at all. I'll feed him and take care of him, I promise. You won't even know there's a dog in the house."

"Hm, if I believed that, I'd believe anything," said Mrs. Clooney.

"He must belong to someone, a handsome dog like that," said Mr. Clooney, his eyes glued to the front window for any sign of Harry. "He's a real thoroughbred."

Harry looked at his father and wagged his tail gratefully.

"Well, I guess he can stay," said Mrs. Clooney, "but we must check the Lost and Found column in the paper. Someone may be looking for him right now. Strange that he's wearing no collar."

"Here comes Harry! But he's not in his suit!" exclaimed Mr. Clooney suddenly. "I guess he must have taken it off. Anyway, his bag is so full he can hardly lift it."

"Thank heavens he's home!" Mrs. Clooney sighed in relief. "Halloween is one night I'm always glad to see end."

The front door swung wide, and in burst Hepzibah the Hateful, disguised from head to toe as Harry Clooney.

"Wait till you see what I got," she gloated in Harry's voice as she set his bag down on the living-room floor.

The real Harry, hidden inside the dog

skin, could only gape at Hepzibah in disbelief. He felt as though he were looking at his own reflection in a mirror, but a reflection that could suddenly walk and talk all by itself.

Why had the witch decided to follow him home anyway? Why hadn't she just left his form hanging in the cupboard with all the rest of her terrible trophies? Whatever the reason, her presence in the house could only spell trouble for his family, of that Harry was certain.

I can't let her stay here, he thought grimly. I've got to drive her away before she puts a spell on the whole family. He took a threatening step forward, his upper lip curled back to reveal a row of long, pointed teeth, and he was absolutely amazed to hear the low, menacing growl that came from his throat.

"Ssh, calm down, boy," whispered Lolly,

putting an anxious hand on his head. "It's just Harry. He lives here too."

"Wow, where did that funny-looking mutt come from?" asked Hepzibah in her new boy's voice. She stepped toward Harry, who snarled again and tried to free himself from Lolly's restraining hand.

"Here, here, we can't have a vicious dog in the house." Mr. Clooney frowned. "Lolly, maybe you'd better put him outside."

"Yeah, I think we should get rid of him," agreed Hepzibah. "I don't like his looks. Besides, he's probably full of fleas."

"Oh, no, Dad," Lolly pleaded. "He'll be good, I know he will. It's just that he's not used to us yet!"

"Funny that he shouldn't like Harry," mused Mrs. Clooney. "Dogs usually adore him."

Harry looked beseechingly from his mother to his father. Please let me stay, he asked them silently. I've got to be here to protect you. Besides, if you put me out, I could end up in the pound.

"Well, we'll give him another chance," decided Mr. Clooney, looking sternly at Harry. "But one more snarl and he's had it." He turned his stern look on Hepzibah. "You're a half hour late coming home, buddy," he said. "I think you'd just better go on upstairs to bed and leave your loot down here."

"Can't I even show you guys what I got?" Hepzibah asked, flopping down on the floor next to the trick-or-treat bag. Carefully she tilted the bag sideways, shaking out some choice pieces of candy.

"Any chocolate-covered marshmallows?" Mr. Clooney asked in spite of himself.

"Plenty," Hepzibah assured him, and the next minute the whole family was sitting in a circle on the floor eating Harry's candy.

Harry stood in back of Lolly, nudging her elbow with his nose.

"No, no, candy would make the doggie sick," she told him. "Tomorrow I'll buy you your very own box of dog biscuits." And if that wasn't bad enough, she added a moment or so later, in a voice thick with caramel fudge, "I think we should call our poodle Maurice." Trust Lolly to pick out a really queer name, Harry thought in annoyance. But as he watched his family devouring his candy, he realized sadly that the only name in the world that would ever suit him was the one that had just been so cruelly stolen from him by the witch.

Later, when everyone headed upstairs for bed, Harry went too. He tried to get into his own room, but Hepzibah barred his way.

"This is my pad now, buster," she said. "You'll have to find yourself another spot."

So Harry settled down for the night under

Lolly's bed. It was rather nice there—dark and quiet and very private. But just as he was dozing off, he thought he heard a scuffling sound out on the lawn. Quickly he wriggled out from under the bed and hurried to the window. By placing his front paws on the sill, he could look down into the moon-flooded backyard below. There in the middle of the lawn was Hepzibah, clad in Harry's plaid pajamas. She was dancing in slow circles, and chanting something in a high, thin wail that didn't sound at all like Harry's voice. Straining his ears, he could just make out her words:

"Moon shine high,
Moon shine low,
Never again will the nasty wind blow."

What in the world did that mean? Was Hepzibah weaving another awful spell out there in the dark? Trembling with appre-

48

hension, Harry crawled back under Lolly's bed and buried his nose between his paws. How could his life have fallen apart so completely and so fast he asked himself. There seemed nothing left now but a lot of frightening questions for which there were no answers. Harry closed his eyes and heaved a troubled sigh. Maybe it was all just a bad dream. Maybe, by tomorrow, things would be all right again. But as he closed his eyes, he knew very well that more than a little cheerful daylight was needed to rescue him from his dreadful predicament.

Next morning, as soon as Lolly opened her bedroom door, Harry was out in the hall like a shot, frantic to see what damage Hepzibah had done to his room during the night. The door stood open, and Harry could see clothes strewn here and there, some of his games pulled down from the bookshelf, and one of his airplane models smashed on the floor. Suddenly his eye lit on the hamster cage in the corner. To his horror, he discovered that Hepzibah had used the new poster paints to turn his hamster orange with purple whiskers. Poor little Herbie was pedaling frantically on his wheel, his fur all sticky and matted. Lolly, who happened to be passing by on her way to the bathroom, let out a squeal when she saw the hamster. She squealed again when she saw what Hepzibah had written on the bathroom mirror.

"I'm telling," she cried, and rushed downstairs to find her mother.

"I don't believe you're starting off the day like this," said Mrs. Clooney to Hepzibah, who was noisily kicking the table leg with her toe as she ate her Shredded Wheat. Harry was eating cereal too from a bowl on the floor. It was rather fun eating down there. He had never had such an interesting view of chair legs before, and he could slurp as much as he wished without anyone telling him to mind his manners.

"You're lucky your father's already left for work," Mrs. Clooney said to Hepzibah. "You'd be grounded for a month if he knew that you'd deliberately slopped paint all over your poor little Herbie and then scribbled on the bathroom mirror as well."

Harry looked up nervously from his cereal bowl. As much as he'd like to see Hepzibah punished, he hoped neither of his parents would do anything to arouse her anger. Goodness only knew what she'd do to them in return. But to his surprise, Hepzibah jumped up from the table, grabbed Harry's snappy new warm-up jacket from the back of her chair, and planted a big kiss on Mrs. Clooney's cheek.

"Don't think you can butter me up that way," Mrs. Clooney warned, but Harry thought her voice sounded a little less stern.

"I want you home immediately after school to give Herbie a bath and to wash off the mirror. Understand?"

"Okay, Mom," Hepzibah agreed cheerfully. She scooped up Harry's lunch box and ran out the kitchen door with Harry at her heels.

"Get away from me, you pesky poodle," she hissed over her shoulder, as Harry followed her down the driveway. But Harry was determined to get to school too. He felt personally responsible for the safety of his entire class, for he had, with that one foolhardy knock on the witch's door, placed every pupil in Mrs. Raymond's third grade in the gravest of danger.

# CHAPTER THREE

# HEPZIBAH
# THE SCHOOL BOY

epzibah and Harry arrived at school just as the eight fifty-five bell sounded. The witch, chortling with anticipation, rushed to join the other students who were streaming into the building through the side door.

"Move, stupid," she ordered a little girl in front of her, and "Out of my way, you turkey," she said to a boy who was blocking her path. Harry, at her side, groaned inwardly. By the end of the day the new Harry Clooney would become the most unpopular student in school, he was sure.

In the hallway, by the water fountain, Harry spotted the Goodhue twins. When they saw Hepzibah, they came running toward her breathlessly, even though running in the halls was strictly forbidden.

"Hey, Clooney, what was the Blackburn house like?" they asked in one voice.

"It was terrific!" Hepzibah told them. "This really nice lady came to the door and asked me in, and you should have seen her candy. Oh, man, it was the greatest! I filled my whole bag right up to the top. It was so heavy I could hardly drag it home."

"What kinds of candy did you get?" Peter Goodhue asked. He and his brother, listening enviously to Hepzibah's mouthwatering answer, hardly noticed Harry, who trailed forlornly after them toward their classroom.

Harry's teacher, Mrs. Raymond, was very nice about letting a dog into the classroom. Of course, she never suspected the big black poodle was really one of her pupils. She allowed him to sit by her desk all morning, and every once in a while she reached down and scratched him fondly behind the ear. The only time Harry got into trouble was during social studies, when Mrs. Raymond called on Hepzibah to name a famous chief of the Apache Indian tribe. The witch stared blankly at the teacher.

"Name a what of the who?" she asked, looking around with a grin at the other pupils.

Mrs. Raymond regarded Hepzibah in surprise. "It's not like you to be so flip, Harry," she said reprovingly. And she turned to Lawrence Whittle, who didn't have the answer either. Harry began to squirm impatiently.

Geronimo, it's Geronimo, he thought, and when Bill Winkleman came up with a wrong answer, Harry could not contain himself a

moment longer. He stood up and enthusias-
tically barked out the answer.

Mrs. Raymond glanced down at him with
a frown. "Ssh," she said, raising a warning
finger to her lips. "If you're not a good doggie, we'll have to ask you to leave." Harry
gave her an apologetic look and settled back
down at her feet with a sigh.

It *is* Geronimo, though, he thought sadly.
And I know the name of another Apache
chief too—Cochise.

Hepzibah's behavior that morning was, as
Harry knew it would be, outrageous. She
was sneaky and just fast enough that Mrs.
Raymond, though often suspicious, was un-
able to catch her at anything. Harry
watched in disgust as Hepzibah went
scampering here and there, sticking her nose
into everybody's business.

She moves like a dumb girl, he thought to
himself, even if she is dressed up in my skin.
Can't they all see I would never skitter

around like that? Even her voice seemed higher than his when she asked for the third time in half an hour to be allowed to get a drink at the water fountain.

"Absolutely not," Mrs. Raymond said, shaking her head. "What is it this morning with you, Harry? All this running around, bothering everyone in the class. I want you to take your seat, please, at once."

With an impudent grin, Hepzibah dawdled to her desk, but the minute Mrs. Raymond turned her attention to someone else Hepzibah leaned over and spit into the Christmas cactus on the windowsill. At once its branches went limp and began to turn yellow, much to the delight of Bill Winkleman, who happened to be standing near her.

"Gee, what a neat trick," he said admiringly. "How did you ever do it?"

Then just before lunch, when Mrs. Raymond had her back turned, Hepzibah threw Marilyn Onderdonk's gym sneaker into the fish tank, sending the zebra fish darting about in agitation and turning the angelfish pale with fright.

As for Harry, though he winced at each new outrage of Hepzibah's, he had never been more popular than he was now in his poodle shape. Everybody made a great fuss over him, and he found when the class went outside for recess that with two extra legs he could easily outrun all his friends. However, not being able to hang by his heels from the jungle gym or play ball with the other boys made him sad. Once, when no one was looking, Hepzibah threw a stone at him, grazing his ear, but Harry got back at her by darting under her heels as she was running to catch a ball. Seeing the witch crash to the ground was delightful, though he couldn't help being sorry that she had torn a hole in the elbow of the new warm-up jacket.

"I'll get you for this, you mangy mongrel," Hepzibah snarled, as she picked herself up. "You just wait and see if I don't."

But Harry, giving the witch a sly nip on the wrist, pranced out of her reach and hurried away with wagging tail after his friend Peter Goodhue.

When school was dismissed at three o'clock, Hepzibah, despite Mrs. Clooney's command to come straight home, went running through the playground in the opposite direction.

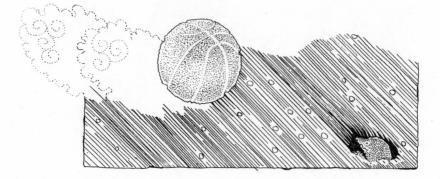

I should see what she's up to, Harry thought worriedly, but he was so weary from his strange, trying day in class that instead of following Hepzibah he decided to wait for Lolly.

"It's nice to have someone to walk home with," Lolly said, when she saw him sitting on the school steps. "I'm going to ask Mom if we can buy you a pretty red collar this afternoon."

Harry began wagging his tail, not because he liked the idea of a collar, but because he suddenly remembered that Hepzibah, not he, would have to hand in the science report that Mrs. Raymond had assigned that afternoon. The class was studying weather, and Hepzibah had immediately asked to be allowed to choose wind as her special subject.

"Oh, boy, do I know a lot about big blows," she boasted. "Wow, wait till you guys all hear my report."

"You have almost a month, class, in which to prepare your assignments," Mrs. Raymond had said, looking at Hepzibah with a puzzled frown. "It will be due the Monday after Thanksgiving." And she had marked the date on her calendar with a big red circle. Harry couldn't understand why Hepzibah was so enthusiastic about having to hand in a science report, but as he trotted along at Lolly's heels he felt certain that anything that gave the witch pleasure was sure to be bad news for someone else.

"What's happened to Harry?" Mrs. Clooney demanded, as Lolly and Harry trooped into the kitchen a few minutes later. "He was supposed to come home right after school to give the hamster a bath."

"We saw him heading toward Swift's Lane," said Lolly. "He was hurrying as though he had something important to do."

Mrs. Clooney shook her head helplessly.

"I don't know what to think," she said. "Ever since he walked into the house last night, he's been a changed boy. And for no reason! What's happened to him anyway?"

"Guess what?" said Hepzibah that night at dinner. "Maurice wormed his way into my classroom today, and when no one was looking, he chewed up the math tests, and then he piddled in the reading corner, and Mrs. Raymond said if we don't keep him at home she's gonna call the dogcatcher."

"My Lord," said Mrs. Clooney, "I had no idea Maurice was at school today. Please apologize to Mrs. Raymond for me, Harry, and assure her that from now on we'll keep him tied."

Harry could hardly believe his ears. He was so indignant at Hepzibah's lies and at the prospect of being tied that he came out from under the dining-room table, barking furiously.

"Lolly, put the dog in the kitchen," ordered Mr. Clooney in annoyance. "We can't have him disrupting our meal like this." With his tail between his legs, Harry was led into the kitchen where he sat by the refrigerator, bitter and frustrated, thinking of all the things he'd like to do to Hepzibah.

The next day, to Harry's great humiliation, Lolly tied him to the maple tree in the backyard.

"I'm sorry, Maurice," she said, kissing the top of his head. "I'll take you for a walk right after school."

Frantically Harry twisted this way and that, winding his rope tighter and tighter around the tree trunk till he could hardly move at all. Luckily, however, Lolly tied poor knots, and in less than fifteen minutes he had managed to free himself. At once he bounded off to school at a gallop. On the

way, a collie tried to get him to play, and a
dachshund nipped at his heels, but Harry
ignored them both. He had better things to
do than pass the time with other dogs.

When he arrived at school, Mr. Zenko,
the janitor, was coming out of a rear door,
carrying a huge garbage pail. Determinedly
Harry wedged himself past Mr. Zenko and
trotted down the hall to Mrs. Raymond's
class. As he was about to scratch for admit-

tance, the door opened and Laurie Hollen-
beck emerged with a jar full of paintbrushes
she was taking to the girls' room to rinse out.
Harry squeezed by her, and was just in time
to catch Hepzibah slyly removing Mrs.
Raymond's purse from her desk. With a
shrill bark, Harry bounded toward the
witch, causing her to drop the purse in
alarm. Mrs. Raymond, who had been at the
back of the room tacking artwork to the bul-
letin board, turned around as her keys, com-
pact, wallet, and comb clattered to the
floor.

"Harry," she cried shrilly, rushing up the
aisle toward Hepzibah, "how dare you go
into my bag? That is an absolutely, unfor-
givably sneaky thing to do! Now you get
down on your hands and knees this minute
and pick everything up."

The rest of the class watched in fascination as Hepzibah, glowering at Mrs. Ray-

mond, reluctantly knelt down and began gathering up the contents of the purse.

Suddenly Marilyn Onderdonk gave a scream. "Yuck, what's that?" she yelled, pointing to something lying on the floor next to Mrs. Raymond's billfold.

Everybody bent to look closer.

"Why, it appears to be a garter snake, minus the head," Mrs. Raymond said in a pleasant, controlled voice. But her expression was far from pleased as she glanced from the shriveled body of the snake to Harry.

"You were planning to dump that thing into my bag, I presume?" she asked him icily.

Harry shrugged and shuffled his feet and grinned and frowned and scratched his nose.

"Well, I think the time has come for a visit to headquarters," Mrs. Raymond declared. She grabbed Harry by the arm and led him, none too gently, toward the door. "And a conference with your mother is also in order," she added, as she marched Harry forcibly down the hall to the principal's office.

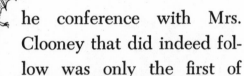

# CHAPTER FOUR

# THE CLOONEYS' ORDEAL

The conference with Mrs. Clooney that did indeed follow was only the first of several. Every day Hepzibah got into some new mischief; if she wasn't terrorizing the younger children in the school, she was throwing food in the lunchroom, ripping pages from books in the library, scribbling words on the blackboard that made Mrs. Raymond, who was no prude, blush profusely. One day Mr. Clooney came home early from work so he could accompany Mrs. Clooney to school.

"Did Mrs. Raymond tell you about Harry and the bat?" asked Lolly, when her parents returned home from their conference, grim and unhappy.

Mrs. Clooney looked startled. "How do you know about that?" she asked.

"The whole school knows," said Lolly with a shrug. "The whole school is talking about how every time my weirdo brother walks into the science room, Mr. Platnik's bat flies down from the ceiling straight into his arms." She turned to Hepzibah, who was standing next to her, grinning at Mr. and Mrs. Clooney. "He actually cuddles that disgusting animal and holds it up against his cheek," Lolly said with a shudder.

Mr. Clooney sat down on the edge of the sofa without even bothering to take off his coat. "Harry, I—er, never knew you were so fond of bats," he said, trying to keep his voice unconcerned and matter-of-fact.

"I like all rodents," Hepzibah said, "a lot."

"Bats are not rodents," Lolly informed him with a superior smile. "They belong to the order Chiroptera. We just learned that in science."

"Well, why do you have to go after a bat anyway, when you have little Herbie upstairs, not to mention our sweet Maurice?" Mrs. Clooney asked. She reached out to pat Harry, who had trotted anxiously into the living room as soon as he heard his parents' car drive into the garage.

"Herbie is a clunk, and dogs are dumb," said Hepzibah in a bored voice. "Bats are better. They're high fliers, and they live in caves, and they have lots of neat little insects stuck in their fur, and they make this really cute squeak, especially when there's a whole flock around. And, best of all, some of 'em like to drink blood."

Mr. Clooney got up abruptly from the

sofa and strode agitatedly across the room. "I don't know what kind of son you're raising here, Bea," he said, glaring at Mrs. Clooney.

"Oh, now I'm the one to blame," said Mrs. Clooney with a bitter laugh. "It's all my fault that our son is turning into a monster."

"No, no, of course it isn't," said Mr. Clooney, looking contrite. "Forgive me, Bea, I don't even know what I'm saying anymore." With a heavy sigh, he sank into his reclining chair. Just the day before, however, Hepzibah had cleverly adjusted the lever on the arm so that now when he sat in it, the headrest sank back precipitously to the floor while the footrest sent his long legs shooting into the air.

"Well, don't all just stand there! Someone help me out of this thing!" Mr. Clooney sputtered furiously, struggling to get up.

"Oh, dear!" murmured Mrs. Clooney, running to his rescue.

"Oh, gosh!" exclaimed Lolly, looking helplessly at her father.

"He looks like a turtle that's been tipped over on his back," commented Hepzibah. She leaned down and whispered gleefully in Harry's ear, "Chalk up one more win, dog boy, for the wonderful, witty, will-o'-the-wisp witch."

If Mr. and Mrs. Clooney's lives were slowly being wrecked by the witch they thought was their son, the real Harry's life wasn't much easier. The only bright spot was the fact that since the handbag incident Mrs. Raymond had welcomed his presence in the classroom.

"If it were not for your wonderful dog keeping watch over us here at school, I don't know, quite frankly, what we'd do," Mrs. Raymond told Harry's mother. "In the last twenty-four hours, he's caught Harry dumping the shavings from the pencil sharpener into Ronald Oberg's lunch bag and sticking a big wad of bubblegum on the back of Laura Wilk's new down vest."

Harry's constant vigilance over her activities simply infuriated Hepzibah.

"There are times when I think maybe I should get rid of you altogether," she told him one Tuesday afternoon, as he was following her home from school. "Of course, as you're already bewitched, I can't put another spell on you, but I could maybe think of a way to get you kicked out of the house into the dog pound."

Hepzibah looked thoughtfully at Harry. "On the other hand, I like to keep a victim around for a while so he can see me at work. In fact, that's practically the best part of stealing someone's shape, letting them see all the cute and clever tricks I pull when I'm inside their silly skins. Not," she added hastily, "that my work is all fun and games, oh no!

Pretending to be someone else is hard work. It takes skill and imagination and patience. Oh, I know some people think being a witch is flying here and there on a broomstick, stirring a big cauldron, putting in an appearance only on Halloween. Well, it's much more than that, if you're a good working witch like myself. When I'm on a case," she told Harry, "I work seven days a week, with no time off. I see a job through to the end, you can bet on that."

A self-satisfied smile spread slowly over her face. "Do you see how I'm managing to disrupt your class?" she asked him. "Do you see how I distract all the students and drive Mrs. Raymond crazy? Do you notice how cleverly I'm getting to your parents and to Lolly too? That is the work of a talented, dedicated witch. You won't catch Hepzibah flying off until she's caused maximum misery, no siree."

Hepzibah turned suddenly to watch a group of boys who were trying unsuccessfully to launch a kite in the windless sky. "Jerks, beetlebrains," she jeered, as the kite kept tumbling to the ground. "Don't they know you can't fly one of those things without a little breeze?" She turned to Harry with an expression of mock concern. "Where do you suppose that wicked old wind went?" she asked him. "Where in the world is he hiding?" And then with an exultant laugh, she ran off at breakneck speed in the direction of Swift's Lane.

Harry, feeling sure she was heading for the Blackburn place, bounded after her, his long, tasseled ears streaming out in back of him. It was not likely Hepzibah would let him in the house; in fact, he had never tried very hard to gain admission, for the place still frightened the wits out of him. But often he stood at the bottom of the porch steps, listening and watching for signs of danger.

What happened one evening several nights later did nothing to calm Harry's fears. Hepzibah had been sent to her room for sticking thumbtacks through the eyes of Lolly's Bucky Dent poster, and Harry was lying outside her door to be sure the witch didn't escape. His ear was cocked for unusual sounds, but when there was only silence from within, he grew drowsy and after a while fell asleep. He was awakened a few minutes later by strange thumpings from his mother's bedroom. Reproaching himself for having dozed off, Harry padded down the hall and pushed open her door with his nose. The room was empty, but Harry had the uneasy feeling he was not alone. Suspiciously he peered into his mother's closet; from among the dresses hanging there, a familiar grinning face looked out at him.

"Gotcha!" said Hepzibah. Over her T-shirt and jeans she was wearing his mother's new flowered silk. On her head was Mrs. Clooney's blond wig. "Call me Mom," she said with a laugh and swaggered across the room. From Mrs. Clooney's jewelry box, she drew forth a strand of pearls, which she looped around her neck. Then playfully she turned the wig around backward on her head. "What kind of mother do you think I'd make anyway?" she inquired with a twinkle in her eye. "Personally, I think a witch in a mother's mask would be a great idea. Can't you just see me messing up car pools and breaking up PTA meetings? Oh, it would be a laugh a minute."

Harry jumped to his feet in agitation. "Don't you dare try to steal my mom's skin," he snarled. "I'll kill you if you try. I swear I will."

Lolly, her eyes swollen and red from the

tears she had shed over Bucky Dent, appeared in Mrs. Clooney's doorway. "Are you okay, Maurice?" she asked. "I heard you growling." When she saw Hepzibah decked out in her mother's wig, she let out a yelp. "Well, now I know you've gone nuts, Harry Clooney," she declared.

Harry winced. He looked with loathing at the grinning Hepzibah. "I'll get even with her yet," he promised himself. "Somehow, some way, I'm going to move her out of here and get my own skin back too." But how he was to accomplish this feat, Harry had no idea.

Thanksgiving came and went, miserably. The Clooneys were in the habit of inviting their next-door neighbors, the Wilsons, to share their turkey, but this year Mrs. Clooney decided the strain of guests would be too great with Harry around. As it was, she overcooked her bird, scorched the carrots, and forgot to add the nuts to her pecan pie. Hepzibah gorged herself with turkey and was later discovered to have carried off the carcass to bed for a midnight snack. Harry, who adored turkey, was given only a few scraps from his mother's plate and some of the skin; as he chomped his meager fare, he reflected sadly that ahead of him loomed Christmas, with even greater disappointments and deprivations in store.

On the Sunday night after Thanksgiving, as Harry was on his way to bed in Lolly's room, Hepzibah stepped from her room with a book in one hand. Harry recognized it as the one on weather Mrs. Raymond had helped her find in the school library.

"It's no wonder all you kids at Hindley Elementary are so dumb," Hepzibah said, waving the book in Harry's face. "Listen to this." She opened to the first page and scornfully began reading aloud: "The faster the wind blows, the sooner we will have a change in the weather." Glancing up from the book, she gave Harry a sly smirk. "Well, don't hold your breath waiting for that change," she advised, "because there's not likely to be one ever again."

Harry wondered uneasily what the witch knew about the weather that the rest of them didn't. He tried to step past her, but she moved quickly into his path. "Listen to this junk," she commanded, turning to the next page. "Clouds that are curled or tufted are named cirrus clouds." Hepzibah shook her head in disgust. "Any idiot knows they are called witch's broom." Taking careful aim, she threw the book over the banister, watching with satisfaction as it plummeted into Mrs. Clooney's dried flower arrangement on the hall table below.

"I've about had it with third grade if you want to know," she confided to Harry. "Many more days with all you klutzes, and

I'll be ready for the funny farm. Tomorrow after I give my science report I'm moving on out."

Harry looked at her in astonishment. Could it be true? Did the witch really mean to leave them? But Hepzibah immediately made her intention all too clear. "Don't worry, I'm not about to run out on the Clooney family," she assured him. "Just planning to switch roles is all." Slowly she reached into the pocket of her jeans and drew out Mrs. Clooney's pearl necklace. "Before you know it, Mom Clooney," she murmured, gently stroking the beads, "you're going to be wearing a new skin. Lolly, love, you're getting a new mom. And Dad Clooney, you're getting a new wife. Hoopla, what fun!" Exploding into laughter, Hepzibah skipped backward into her room and slammed the door behind her.

If Harry had been able to fall to his knees

and pray, he would certainly have done so then. The best he could manage, however, was to sit up on his hindquarters and howl. Lolly came rushing from her room, sure that Hepzibah was killing her precious dog. Mr. and Mrs. Clooney rushed from the den, thinking Maurice might be trying to warn them of some new outrage being committed by their son. None of them knew that the howl was really a cry for help, a plea for a miracle to save them all from the ruthless witch.

# CHAPTER FIVE

# HEPZIBAH READS HER REPORT

**W**ho is ready to read his report to the class?" Mrs. Raymond asked at the beginning of science period next day.

"I am, I am!" cried Hepzibah, wriggling eagerly in her seat.

"Very well, Harry," said Mrs. Raymond. "I think you told me that your title was to be 'Why the Wind Blows.'"

"I've changed it," said Hepzibah, rising to her feet. "Now it's called 'Why the Wind Doesn't Blow.'"

The witch cleared her throat and began

to read: "Everybody knows the wind is bad. It uproots trees you could have used for hiding in. It topples chimneys you planned to slip down in order to spy on people. It blows your cape off the clothesline. It drives smugglers' ships up on the rocks." Here Hepzibah paused and looked significantly at the class. "It can even blow you away if you're not careful."

There was a moment of puzzled silence. Then Eric Goodhue, with a grin on his face, asked, "Did the wind try to drag you out to sea or something, Clooney?"

"Quiet, class," cautioned Mrs. Raymond, as several students began to giggle.

Hepzibah looked at Eric through narrowed eyes. "How did you know?" she demanded suspiciously.

"Know what?" asked Eric.

"About what the wind tried to do to me this summer."

Lawrence Whittle burst out laughing. "Oh, come on, Clooney," he said, "you're really acting like a jerk."

Hepzibah, ignoring his remark, closed her eyes for a moment, as if trying to recall all the details of a terrible ordeal. She placed her report face down on her desk and began to speak very slowly.

"I was at the beach this summer," she told the class, "standing at the edge of the sea. It was a very dangerous thing for me to have done, to go on the beach, because I don't swim, and the wind knows that. But it was such a beautiful day that I couldn't resist. The sky was gray, and the water was gray. You could hardly tell where one ended and the other began. And there was a fog rolling off the ocean. I thought to myself, even if the wind is lurking around somewhere, he'll never be able to see me through the mist. Besides, there were a lot of big rocks just off the shore, and I was hoping to see a ship-wreck. Well, all of a sudden, there was a terrible roar in back of me, like a freight train, and the next thing I knew I had been swept out to sea! I was blown over the tops of the waves, head over heels, like a giant beach ball. Now if the wind had suddenly stopped blowing, I would have sunk to the bottom of the ocean; it would have been the end for me. But, dummy that he is, the wind was having so much fun showing off that he just kept huffing and puffing away, which kept me on top of the waves instead of underneath them. Anyway, out I went, into the middle of the ocean. Once I made a grab at a periscope sticking up in the water and held on for dear life, but the wind tore it from my grasp and sent me bowling farther and farther out to sea. And then, about a hundred miles from shore, when the fog had gotten thick as cotton candy and that billowy buffoon couldn't see what he was doing, he blew me up on the deck of a ship. Before he could lift me off again, I ran down into the ship's hold and stayed there in hiding till we docked a couple of days later."

The class was absolutely still. All eyes, including Mrs. Raymond's, were turned in fascination upon Hepzibah.

"I don't believe what I'm hearing," the real Harry, who was sitting beside the teacher's desk, heard Mrs. Raymond mutter. "That child gets nuttier every day."

Then a girl named Harriet Pearce spoke up. "But the wind does good things too," she reminded them all. "It helps our soil. It carries seeds—"

"Don't interrupt!" Hepzibah snapped, glowering at Harriet. "I'm not finished."

She continued reading from her report. "Now the wind no longer blows, and this is the reason why." A smile of satisfaction crept slowly over her face. "A force," she read, speaking loudly so no one would miss a word, "a force stronger and more powerful, craftier and more cunning than the wind at his wildest bottled up that gusty clown on Labor Day weekend as he lay snoozing behind a pine tree." Hepzibah looked around the room in triumph and then flopped down into her seat.

The class and the teacher, thoroughly mystified, stared at her in amazement.

"Is that it?" asked Mrs. Raymond in wonder.

"But what was the powerful force that bottled up the wind?" Lawrence Whittle demanded.

"That's for me to know and for you to find out," said Hepzibah.

Mrs. Raymond shook her head and sighed. "Well, Harry, your theory about where the wind went is certainly an original

one, but hardly what I'd call a scientific explanation."

The real Harry got up from under the desk and shook himself vigorously. He was not quite as mystified by Hepzibah's report as the rest of the class. He felt pretty certain who that powerful force was that she had described. The witch herself had trapped the wind. He was sure of it. But the next question was: where had she hidden it? And then suddenly, like a light flashing on inside his head, Harry thought of the strange glass globe of swirling snow he had seen in Hepzibah's house on Halloween night. Could that possibly be where the wind was imprisoned? But of course it was! The more Harry thought about it, the more certain he was that he had hit upon the secret hiding place. The trouble was, though, how could he, in his present poodle shape, possibly tell anyone of his discovery?

"If I could just get hold of that ball," he told himself, "and smash it to pieces, I know I could free the wind. Then he would really go after Hepzibah. He'd really give it to her after what she's done to him." But it wasn't just the thought of seeing Hepzibah punished that was so exhilarating; if the witch was busy protecting herself from a wrathful wind, she would have no time to hurt his mother or anyone else in his family. Of course, that was all well and good, but it still wasn't going to help him get back his own shape again, not unless— Harry suddenly began to pant with excitement, for a stupendous idea had occurred to him, and for the first time he was sure that he had a chance of outwitting the witch. Harry was so overcome with the possibility of salvation that he threw back his head and let out a loud bark.

"Oh, oh, I think Maurice needs to go out," said Mrs. Raymond. Rising quickly from her desk, she took hold of Harry's collar and led him out of the classroom.

"There's a good boy," she said, holding open the door at the end of the hall with one hand and pushing Harry through with the other. "Your friends will be out in a little while." And she shut the door firmly behind him.

# CHAPTER SIX

# REVENGE

arry settled down on the uncomfortable metal doormat. He would just have to wait there till school was dismissed. He was hopeful that Hepzibah would head for the Blackburn place as she usually did on Friday afternoons. Until he was able to get inside that house of hers and lay hold of the glass globe, there was no possible way to put his plan for saving himself and his mother into action.

Time moved with excruciating slowness. He watched two squirrels chasing each

101

other through the bare branches of an oak tree. He observed a flock of wild geese flying in formation over the school. He looked without interest at a boy and girl playfully pushing each other into a privet hedge on their way home from the high school. And then, as the clock in the town hall struck three, the dismissal bell rang loud and clear. Harry, listening for the sounds of running feet inside the school, found himself trembling from head to paw, partly from cold, partly from nerves. He didn't have long to wait. Hepzibah was one of the first pupils to come bursting through the door. Pausing only long enough to make a face at him and to hurl a few insults at some second graders, she went rushing across the school grounds in the direction of Swift's Lane. Harry hurried after her, ducking behind trees whenever Hepzibah glanced back over her shoulder. It wouldn't do to let the witch see him too soon, Harry thought, for knowing she was being spied on would make her even more ornery than usual, and she would never let him into her house. As it was, she might not let him in anyway and then he would be in trouble. But Harry was counting on a combination of his own quickness and Hepzibah's vanity. He knew how the witch loved to flaunt her cruel schemes before an audience; he just prayed she was in one of her show-off moods today.

Harry waited in back of a willow tree till he saw the witch run up the front steps of the Blackburn place and reach under the doormat for the key. As soon as she had let herself into the house, he trotted up onto the porch and bravely scratched at the door. Although he could no longer reach the cat knocker, the bewhiskered head meowed mournfully anyway. Harry looked up at it with sympathy, wondering what poor unfortunate creature was imprisoned in back of the gloomy, brass face. Then he heard footsteps inside the house. Slowly the front door creaked open, and before Hepzibah had a chance to shoo him away, Harry slipped past her and was prancing expectantly toward the hall table where the glass globe had rested on Halloween night. To his bitter disappointment, however, it was no longer there! Harry stared at the empty tabletop in despair, his glorious vision of snatching the globe triumphantly in his teeth rapidly fading to nothing.

"How dare you follow me, you flea-bitten cur!" Hepzibah hissed. "Go home, get lost, get out of my sight!"

But Harry was not ready to give up yet. Ignoring Hepzibah's command, he turned and trotted down the hall toward the kitchen, his toenails clicking briskly on the bare floor. The globe had to be somewhere in this house, and the kitchen seemed a logical spot to begin his search.

"Oh, all right, I suppose you can stay for a few minutes, you old snoop," Hepzibah grumbled, following along in back of Harry. "I was just about to feed the bird." She looked up at the parrot, sitting on top of the kitchen cupboard. "He's an antique, you know. I stole his pirate skin back in 1580. What a fun year that was!" Hepzibah reached into a bread box on the kitchen counter and drew out a hard, white biscuit, which she waved toward the parrot. Immediately he swooped down and snatched it greedily from her hand in his powerful beak.

"You should have seen me prancing around as a pirate," she said, a dreamy look stealing over her face. "What a beautiful buccaneer I was! What a clever corsair, what a rollicking rover." She closed the bread box with a bang. The dreamy look disappeared. "It's time to slip into something more comfortable," she announced, moving toward the cupboard in which she kept her disguises. She took a key out of her jeans pocket, quickly unlocked the cupboard door, and lifted the limp Hepzibah shape from its peg.

"Remember this?" she said, smoothing the folds of the long, musty cape. She frowned as she looked at the cape's bulging pockets. "I certainly do manage to accumulate a lot of stuff," she sighed, pulling forth a compass, a slingshot, a few candy corns, which she laid on the kitchen table. From another pocket she pulled out some baseball trading cards and crumpled Kleenex. And then from a third pocket out came— Could it be? Yes it was—the glass globe with the snow circling inside it as madly as ever.

"*Regardez*," she said, caressing the ball

like a miser fondling his gold. "That's French for 'Get a load of this.' " Gloatingly she held the globe up to the light and in Harry's voice began to chant:

"What once was wild?
What once was free?
What now is mild
and meek as can be?
What once could howl
and shriek and blow
and now can swirl only mini snow?

"Betcha don't know the answer to that one, dog boy!" she cackled.

Betcha I do, thought Harry, every muscle in his body taut with excitement. Hepzibah lowered the globe and placed it on the table next to the slingshot.

"Hang on, here comes Hepzibah!" she cried, whirling the witch's cape about her.

Harry, poised like a runner at the starting

line, dashed to the table the minute the witch disappeared into the cape's billowing folds. Jumping up on his hind legs, he managed to seize the globe in his teeth just as Hepzibah in her own witch body emerged grinning from under the cape, clutching the empty form of Harry Clooney in her hand. But the grin dissolved into a howl of horrified surprise when she discovered the globe bulging from Harry's mouth.

"Give me that thing!" she bellowed, red sparks of rage flying from her eyes. But Harry could tell by her voice that she was as frightened as she was angry.

"If you drop that ball . . ." she warned, but the thought of what might happen was apparently so horrendous she couldn't even finish the sentence.

Now I've got her where I want her, Harry thought to himself, almost choking with excitement. He gave his head a quick little toss to drive the globe farther back in his mouth. Although it was not a large globe, it was slippery, and keeping it firmly anchored was going to be tricky.

He stepped closer to the witch and stared meaningfully down at the lifeless shape in her hand. Seeing his own form dangling there so empty and forlorn made him tremble all over. Yet the bright hope was growing that it might soon be his again.

Hepzibah, following Harry's gaze with a frown, let out a sudden cry of comprehension as it dawned on her what he was trying to ask for.

"I get it!" she exclaimed. "You want to make a trade—the Harry Clooney suit for the glass ball, right?"

For answer, Harry wagged his tail as hard as he could.

Hepzibah stamped her foot angrily. "Out of the question," she snorted. "I never return anyone's body to them, never." She glared at Harry and glared at the globe and muttered and mumbled to herself and fiddled with the end of her cape. Harry, hardly daring to breathe, watched and waited in silence.

Suddenly Hepzibah reached out and punched the cupboard door in frustration. "All right, all right," she snarled. "Maybe just this once I will make an exception. You can't have your own shape back, I'm not finished with it yet, but I'll trade you the ball for some other form." She turned back to the cupboard and peered inside. "What do you fancy?" she asked over her shoulder. "How about this marvelous tramp suit? I'll even throw in some trading cards with it."

For answer, Harry sat down with his back to her.

"Very well, if you're not interested in going through life as a tramp, how about starting all over again with this?" Hepzi-

110

bah drew down the baby and held it up against her. "You put this on, and grown-ups fall all over you," she assured him. "Let out one little peep, and they come running with warm milk and juice and biscuits. You never have to go to school. You never have to pick up your room or do anything you don't want to. You'd love it."

Harry gave the witch a stony look over his shoulder. His jaws were beginning to ache from holding the globe, but no power on earth could ever make him let go of it.

"Why you want to be a child again beats me," the witch said peevishly. "Children are all the same—tiresome and noisy. They smell funny, especially the boys. Their teeth fall out. Their shoelaces come untied. Their temperatures go up. Their socks fall down. They're altogether a mess."

But Harry just stared at the witch, never moving a muscle, looking as if he were prepared to sit there on her kitchen floor till Doomsday if needs be. Hepzibah stared back with a look of hatred and resentment on her face. The kitchen was beginning to fill with shadows as the afternoon sun dipped low in the sky; the clock on the wall ticked away the seconds and then the minutes one by one.

Hepzibah began to fidget and twitch. Once again her impatience got the better of her. "You win," she cried, throwing up her arm in a gesture of defeat. "If you must have your ridiculous skin, here." Unbelievably, she bent down and laid Harry's form at his feet. "Now the ball at once, please," she demanded, holding out her hand.

But Harry stepped away from her. Unless Hepzibah draped the form over his shaggy dog shoulders, it was of no use to him. For he knew the moment he let go of the globe, Hepzibah would grab it in one hand and snatch back his boy shape in the other before he ever had a chance to work his black, furry muzzle under it.

"Now what?" Hepzibah screeched in a frenzy, as Harry sat looking up at her. "I've given you your precious shape. You have to keep your end of the bargain and give me that ball!"

Harry lowered his head and pushed at his form to let Hepzibah know what he wanted. For a moment or two the witch hedged, pretending not to understand. But Harry had the upper hand, and she knew it.

"Whoever would have thought that a cantankerous canine like you could outfox a wonderful witch like me," she fumed. "You drive a hard bargain, sir."

Angrily she flung Harry's form over him like a shawl, and the minute she did so he felt a tingling sensation all over his body.

"The ball, please," he heard Hepzibah demand again, but her voice seemed to be coming from far, far away.

For some reason, he suddenly found he could no longer hold the ball in his teeth. Something seemed to be changing size— either his mouth or the globe. Frantically his paws flew up to catch the ball as it fell. Then miracle of miracles, he saw in front of him not furry paws at all but his own familiar, wonderful hands!

"The spell is broken," he shouted in triumph. "I'm me again. I'm Harry Lewis Clooney, and I'm here to stay!"

In front of him Hepzibah was dancing up and down on her toes like a boxer. "Give me the ball," she commanded, "before I decide to turn you into a toad."

Harry knew he had to act fast. Quickly he raised both hands and sent the ball crashing to the floor.

"You fool!" shrieked Hepzibah, as it shattered into a thousand pieces. "You blithering idiot! Now we're really in for it!"

At once, from out of the fragments of glass, there arose what looked like a slender blue column of smoke. Rapidly it began to spiral upward toward the kitchen ceiling.

"Spiders and toads!" cursed Hepzibah, bracing herself against the cupboard. "I've got to get out of here!"

The spiraling column, whining like a spinning top, quickly billowed out into a fat blue balloon that grew and grew, pressing against the kitchen walls, pushing against the ceiling till the old house groaned and creaked like a ship in a storm. And as the wind swelled, its whine turned into a wild, gleeful howl.

Oh, boy, I better get out too, thought Harry. Lurching and stumbling, grabbing at furniture to keep himself from falling, he half ran, half blew toward the kitchen door.

"See what you've done!" Hepzibah screeched at him. Her hat had blown off; her cape was streaming out in back of her. She stumbled only as far as the kitchen table before being hurled to the floor.

"I'll make you pay for this," she yelled. "I'll make you wish you'd never been born. I'll—" But Harry never heard the end of the witch's threat, for at that moment the wind, like an impatient doorman, suddenly flung open the kitchen door and shoved Harry outside, slamming the door shut in back of him so hard that its glass panes dissolved in a shower of splinters.

Shaking with excitement and fear and relief, Harry picked himself up from the lawn where the wind had pitched him and ran out into Swift's Lane as fast as his two beautiful boy's legs would carry him. He had gone no more than a few yards, however, when he was stopped dead in his tracks by a dreadful ripping, tearing sound behind him. He turned in time to see the Blackburn place being lifted clear off its foundation. Gusts of wind were spurting from the broken windows and spiraling crazily from the chimney.

"Good grief!" exclaimed Harry, as the house, swaying from side to side, circled heavenward. Around and around it spun at a dizzying speed, and Harry thought he saw at one of the windows a witch's face, the mouth contorted in a howl. Looking no bigger than a dollhouse, the Blackburn place, for one brief moment, was silhouetted against the twilight sky before it careered over the edge of the horizon and disappeared from sight.

"Way to go, wind!" shouted Harry, flinging his arms into the air. And then he turned and ran joyfully toward home.

It need hardly be said that Harry's parents were overcome with happiness at having their son back again, although, in fact, they didn't realize he had been missing till he told them his long tale of adventure.

"I knew there was something special about that sweet poodle," crooned Mrs. Clooney, hugging Harry tightly against her. "But I had no idea how special. I had no idea my darling, courageous boy was hidden under all that fur."

"Harry, the hero," murmured Mr. Clooney, his eyes misting with emotion. "Never again will I feel the tug of the wind without remembering your bravery, son. And to think I was about to pack you off to a private school in the country!"

"With the money we'll be saving by keeping Harry at home, can we buy a new dog then?" asked Lolly. "I just can't live without a dog," she told them dramatically. "I might get sick and die if I don't get one right away."

"Well, before we do anything about a new pet, let's go see if there's anything left of the Blackburn place," suggested Mr. Clooney.

So they all put on sweaters and hurried on foot to Swift's Lane. In the relief and excitement of the moment, only Harry remembered that his failure to stay away from the Blackburn place was what had caused his family all those weeks of anguish. "I'll make it up to them," he promised himself, as he strode along beside his father. "I'll get a paper route so I can buy them something extra nice for Christmas."

By the time the Clooneys arrived, the street was streaming with people coming to look at the huge, gaping hole where Hepzibah's house had stood. A police car had even pulled up at the curb, the red light on its roof searching the darkness like a great re-volving eye.

"Must have been a tornado," said a man in the crowd, staring into the empty founda-tion. "That's the way they hit, you know, completely wipe out one building and never touch the one next to it."

"Well, I for one am glad the Blackburn place is gone," declared a woman standing near him. "It was really a terrible eyesore."

Lolly and Harry and most of the other spectators stood with their faces raised to the sky, gratefully feeling the rough caress of the wind which, having spent much of its fury blowing away Hepzibah and her house, was now gusting in circles, tugging at hats, plucking at jackets, and then dashing off like a merry child playing tag.

"You'll have to get a new costume for next year," Lolly said to Harry. "Your poodle suit is probably still on the kitchen floor of the

Blackburn place, heading for Africa, along with the rest of the house."

"I hope so," said Harry earnestly. He suddenly found himself wondering what might have happened if he had appeared at Hepzibah's doorstep on Halloween night dressed as something other than a poodle. Red Raider, in comic books and on TV, spit flames when anyone made him angry. Black Bandit, on the other hand, bored holes in his enemies' brains with a lasar beam that shot out from behind his mask.

I might have set the school on fire or put a hole through Lolly, Harry thought with a shudder. Maybe it was better to have been a poodle, as long as I had to be something strange.

He glanced down at his own hand, admiring the short, rather grubby nails and the Captain Cool special decoding ring on his finger.

"I'm glad not to be any kind of magical person," he said to Lolly. "Life gets too complicated when you can't just be your own self."

"Sometimes it gets complicated anyway," Lolly told him wisely. "I'm hungry. Let's go have supper." She gave her brother a quick tap on the shoulder. "Touched you last," she teased, and tore off down Swift's Lane with Harry right at her heels.

"Don't run, you'll fall in the dark," Mrs. Clooney called after them. But all at once she clapped her hands to her head with a cry of dismay.

"What is it, Bea?" asked Mr. Clooney anxiously.

"My pot roast!" she wailed. "It'll be burned to a crisp!" And quite forgetting her own warning, she set off down the lane at a gallop.

"Wait for me!" called Mr. Clooney running after her. All around them was the wind, busily scattering leaves, whistling among the bare branches of the trees, joyously making up for lost time.

Barbara Dillon was born in Montclair, New Jersey, and received a B.A. degree in English from Brown University. She worked for seven years as an editorial assistant for *The New Yorker* magazine and for five years taught prereading skills to three- and four-year-old children at daycare centers in Stamford, Connecticut.

Mother of three girls, Mrs. Dillon lives with her husband in Darien, Connecticut.

Chris Conover was born in New York City and studied at the High School of Music and Art and at the State University of New York at Buffalo. Since 1974, she has illustrated a number of well-received children's books, including *Six Little Ducks*, which she wrote as well. Currently Ms. Conover lives in Boston, Massachusetts.